KiDS'
Little Instruction
Book S.M.B.S.D. R.I.F.

By Jim & Steve Dodson

Troll

INTRODUCTION

How many kids have dreamed of meeting Shaquille O'Neal, Joe DiMaggio, Tom Brokaw, Chevy Chase, Sandra Day O'Connor, Dan Marino, or George Bush? Our dreams came true when we started working for *Kidzette,* the first newspaper in the United States written by and for children.

As reporters we interviewed many celebrities on a variety of topics. One of our most frequently asked questions was "What advice would you give to children growing up in today's world?" We thought kids might listen to sports heroes and movie stars sooner than they would listen to their parents and teachers. We created a monthly column called "Wise Words to Kids" to share these valuable insights with *Kidzette* readers in Palm Beach County, Florida. The response was overwhelming.

During the past three years, we have conducted hundreds of personal interviews and corresponded with thousands of famous people. The advice we've obtained is so worthwhile, we wanted to share it with kids every-where. *Kids' Little Instruction Book* is a collection of our favorite quotes. We hope you enjoy them.

Jim and Steve

"I'll tell you the same thing my mother used to tell me: 'The most important thing in life is to try to do the very best for your neighbors. Respect other people.'"

Henry "Hank" Aaron
Hall of Fame Outfielder—Atlanta Braves,
All-time Home Run King

"Just remember that nothing is as bad as it seems and nothing is as good as it sometimes appears."

Troy Aikman
Star Quarterback—Dallas Cowboys

"My father was fond of quoting Satchel Paige, who said: 'Don't look back, something may be catching up to you.' Look to the future. . . . There's always a new day tomorrow that will keep you laughing and cheerful."

Jane Alexander
Actress

"Don't avoid pain. It's a part of life. It helps you know you're alive. Rejection, frustration, disappointment, anger, unrequited love . . . it all hurts. And it all heals. So never run from pain. Just run to those who are in it with an open heart."

Jason Alexander
Actor—"Seinfeld"

"Love yourself. Respect yourself. Never sell yourself short. Believe in yourself regardless of what people think. You can accomplish anything, absolutely anything, if you set your mind to it."

Marcus Allen
Star Running Back—Kansas City Chiefs

"A couple of different sayings have always stuck with me and they are:

'A man's most open actions have a secret side to them,' and 'The man who believes he can do it is probably right; and so is the man who believes he can't.'"

Tim Allen
Comedian, Actor—"Home Improvement"

"Education is the foundation for not only success in your future professional life, but your social life as well. Throughout the years of your education, you will forge friendships that will last a lifetime while taking steps that will allow you to overcome any obstacle and contribute to the future of our society."

Peter Angelos
Owner—Baltimore Orioles

"Be respectful to others as you grow. . . . If we lack respect for one group, then there is a tendency for that attitude to spread. It becomes infectious and no one becomes safe from the ravages of prejudice."

Walter Annenberg
Philanthropist, Publisher—*TV Guide*

"Don't consider athletes 'heroes'—they're just athletes. Be an individual—be yourself, not an empty-headed copycat of your peers. Do your own thing—*always*."

Jules Archer
Author

"Shoot for the moon, for even if you don't make it, you will land among the stars."

Mary Kay Ash
Founder—Mary Kay Cosmetics

"Learn from the mistakes of the fools that came before you. Then show the world how smart you are by making original ones."

Ed Asner
Actor

"Believe half of what you see, none of what you hear."

Joe Don Baker
Actor

"Listen to your mother. Mothers are always right."

Brian Baldinger
Football Player—Philadelphia Eagles

"Think positive. . . . Don't let anyone tell you that you can't do something. Just go do it."

Ernie Banks
Baseball Hall of Famer—Chicago Cubs

"Pursue your ideas and never give up."

Joseph Barbera
Co-founder—Hanna-Barbera Productions

"Do NOT spit gum in the drinking fountains."

Dave Barry
Pulitzer Prize-winning Author, Humor Columnist

"Learn all you can about people in other parts of the world. Understanding how people in other countries live and work and play teaches us to respect them and promotes peace everywhere."

Carol Bellamy
Director—Peace Corps,
Former Director—United Nations Childrens' Fund-UNICEF

"Developing curiosity and the instinct for seeking creative solutions are perhaps the most important contributions education can provide. With time, many facts we are asked to learn will be forgotten, but we are less likely to lose our ability to question and discover."

Paul Berg
Nobel Laureate in Chemistry

"We have to recognize and honor even our smallest triumphs, the personal-best goals we have set for ourselves, even if they seem less than noteworthy to others."

Bonnie Blair
Olympic Champion Speedskater

"I'm an observer. I'm always watching and listening. I'm fascinated by people. That's a great way to get ideas."

Judy Blume
Author

"Whatever you decide you really want to do with your life, take it very seriously. . . . You find that by focusing on what you want to do with your life, it happens. And don't let anything take you off course. Commit yourself early on."

Michael Bolton
Singer

"There really is a lot of laughter in this world. Sometimes you have to work for it or you have to be open to it, but it's here. This is a neat planet. Enjoy it."

Erma Bombeck
Humor Columnist, Author

"My father always said to 'Stay in there and pitch!' There are times in our lives when it would be so easy to quit, but persistence is the only way to achieve success."

Frank Borman
Astronaut

"Stay busy with your life. Study hard, go to school, play sports, get a job. But don't just lie around doing nothing. That is when you find trouble to get into."

Bobby Bowden
Football Coach—Florida State University

"I give you some advice that is now more than 2,000 years old: Love work, hate domination, and don't get too close to the ruling class."

Ben Bradlee
Executive Editor—*Washington Post*

"If you listen to anybody but yourself you are a prime sucker. Because all anybody else ever does is make mistakes. Why should you make the same ones? Make your own mistakes. They are the best fun."

Jimmy Breslin
Pulitzer Prize-winning Columnist, Author

"You have the good fortune to be part of a free nation with boundless possibilities—and enough challenges and diversions to make life interesting every day. . . . Read books. Write stories. Learn history. Enjoy life."

David S. Broder
Columnist—*Washington Post,* TV Panelist

"You've got to pay attention to the fundamentals. You *do* have to work hard. You *do* have to study. You *do* have to pay attention to the real things in life. . . . If you just do half of what your parents tell you, you'll probably be twice as far ahead."

Tom Brokaw
Television News Anchor—NBC News

"Think about the world we live in and how we can keep it safe and beautiful. . . . Take part in your communities' Earth Day celebrations and get involved in your schools' environmental activities. Remember, the earth is in your hands!"

Carol Browner
Administrator—U.S. Environmental Protection Agency

"Just a few thoughts: Never pay for a telephone call when you can call collect. Never let anyone see you perspire when you are skiing down a steep hill. Never sit next to a child under two on an airplane. That about does it."

Art Buchwald
Pulitzer Prize-winning Columnist, Author

"In life you are given two ends, one to think with and the other to sit on. Your success in life depends on which end you use most. Heads you win, tails you lose!"

Conrad Burns
United States Senator—Montana

"Keep your imagination alive. It will give you delights your whole life."

James Burrows
Director—"Cheers," "Taxi," and "Frasier"

"I truly believe that our thoughts influence what we experience in life. Do yourself a favor and spend at least one moment today thinking of our world as a safe, healthy, and *wonder full* place to be."

LeVar Burton
Actor

"Life is not a goal, it's a process. You get there step by step by step. If you attempt to make every step wondrous and magical, that's what your life will be."

Leo Buscaglia
Author

"Do everything the best you can. Everything. The key to success is to be the best you can possibly be at every task you encounter and every role you play. By doing this, you prepare yourself for every opportunity."

Barbara Bush
Former First Lady

"Obey your parents. Grow up to be strong. Stay out of the drug scene."

George Bush
Former President of the United States

"Every now and then, without anyone knowing about it, do something kind for someone who needs and doesn't expect it. Things like that circulate the earth in invisible ways and make this planet a better place."

Brett Butler
Comedienne, Actress—"Grace Under Fire"

"Know and take pride in your history and heritage so that your generation is able to make greater strides into the future."

Ben Nighthorse Campbell
United States Senator—Colorado,
First Native American in U.S. Senate

"Anyone has the opportunity to make his life worthwhile. The important thing is to have a goal. You've got to trust your judgment and put your faith in God. Never say never."

Gary Carter
Former Star Catcher—Montreal Expos,
Two-time All-Star Game MVP

"While you are in school, you will encounter learning opportunities that you may never have again. Enjoy them and take advantage of them all! The future of our great nation will soon be in the hands of young people like you."

Jimmy Carter
Former President of the United States

"Decide on a challenging goal, something you would really like to do in your life, then work hard to reach it. And don't let the fear of failure hold you back. It is not a tragedy to strive for something and not achieve it; it is a tragedy to never try."

Rosalynn Carter
Former First Lady

"Have the courage to stay with your own opinion."

David Caruso
Actor

"Make sure when you drive that you always have the airbag inflated."

Chevy Chase
Actor

"Work hard to achieve your goals. . . . If you know where you want your career to go at an early stage in life, you should try and learn as much about that industry as possible."

Liz Claiborne
Fashion Designer

"It has been often said that you can judge a person's worth by the company he keeps."

Eric Clapton
Musician

"In terms of making a living, try to select something you can accomplish. Don't set unreasonable goals for yourself. It's just like deciding to drive across the country to a particular destination. Plan your route. Try your best not to get lost. Press on, and eventually you will reach your destination."

Dick Clark
TV and Radio Personality

"I hope you will follow the advice my mother gave me: Always try to make the world a better place."

Beverly Cleary
Author

"I believe that young people are the future of our country. . . . The most important thing you can do for your country is to work hard in the classroom and prepare yourself for the time when your generation will be leading America. . . . I challenge each of you to take personal responsibility for your future and for the future of America."

Bill Clinton
President of the United States

"Things may come to those who wait, but only the things left by those who hustle."

Dennis Connor
Yachtsman, America's Cup Winner

"After you turn forty years old, never trust anybody with a thirty-one-inch waist."

Bill Cosby
Actor, Comedian

"Don't take anything for granted. Don't be so sure that your parents don't have at least some of the answers."

Bob Costas
Sportscaster

"It may be helpful for you to recall from time to time the saying that my father quoted to me more often than any other: 'In the bright lexicon of youth, there is no such word as *can't*.' Sometimes he expressed the same theme a little differently: 'He started to sing as he tackled the thing that couldn't be done—and he did it.'"

Archibald Cox
Watergate Prosecutor

"Never take the easy way out."

Aaron Craver
Football Player—Denver Broncos

"Care about people, not things. Remember that things can be replaced. People can't."

Judith Crist
Film and Drama Critic

"Have a lifelong interest in reading since reading is the key to knowledge, and knowledge is enlightenment and the ultimate path to success."

Walter Cronkite
Legendary News Anchorman

"Challenge yourself to achieve your full potential."

Nancy Currie
Astronaut

"Trust yourself and your instincts. Try not to be swayed by what others do but concentrate on what you want. *You* are the only *you* around and you are *special*."

Jamie Lee Curtis
Actress

"You can't live without ideas."

Alexandra Danilova
Ballerina

"Cartooning is nice work if you can get it."

Jim Davis
Cartoonist—"Garfield"

"**S**uccess in life is the result of focusing your energies and efforts in a specific direction and using your capabilities to their fullest. And take time to help those less fortunate; it will fill your heart with joy."

Michael DeBakey, M.D.
Cardiac Surgeon

"**T**he greatest assets you own are your dreams. Don't let anybody take them away from you. Associate with others who support your dreams and can help you make them come true. Whatever your dream, always believe that you can do it."

Richard DeVos
Co-Founder—Amway Corporation,
Owner—Orlando Magic

"Approach life with a positive attitude."

Lincoln Diaz-Balart
United States Congressman—Florida

"Keep your feet on the ground, your nose to the grindstone, and your eye on the sky."

Phyllis Diller
Comedienne

"Make sure you get an education. Do what's right in school. Listen to your teachers. You know what to do."

Joe DiMaggio
Baseball Hall of Famer—New York Yankees

"No matter what road you travel in life, try to make a difference, and above all seek excellence not to please the crowd, but because of the standards you set for yourself."

William Donaldson
Chairman and CEO—New York Stock Exchange

"Remember that you can accomplish just about anything in life that you want to accomplish if you focus enough of your energies in that direction. . . . Hard work will always be the key to success."

Tony Dorsett
Former Running Back—Dallas Cowboys,
Heisman Trophy Winner

"Be kind, be decent, be generous, be tolerant, compassionate, and understanding. Be fast to praise, slow to judge. Remember, we're all human, and don't cast the first stone."

Allen Drury
Pulitzer Prize-winning Author

"Follow your heart, your instincts. People might try to dissuade you from your passion, but no one can live your life but you."

Olympia Dukakis
Actress

"My father always taught me to give an honest day's work if I expected an honest day's pay. Today's kids need to apply that principle, whether it be in regards to cutting lawns or just living life."

Joe Dumars
All-Star Guard—Detroit Pistons

"I have found the meaning of the following words true, pertinent, and profitable: 'Hidden in every problem is an opportunity.'. . . The hidden opportunity may seem elusive at first, but it is there. Find it."

Buddy Ebsen
Actor—"Beverly Hillbillies"

"Your time in school is the most important time in your life. . . . Learn all that you can! Everything you learn now will serve you well someday. . . . We all depend upon you young people because one day soon, you will be 'in charge' of the world."

Michael Eisner
CEO—The Walt Disney Company

"Pick the kind of work you enjoy and a goal toward which to direct your energy. Work will then be fun and you will be successful."

Gertrude B. Elion
Nobel Laureate in Medicine

"Find something that you're really interested in doing in your life. Pursue it, set goals, and commit yourself to excellence. Do the best you can."

Chris Evert
Tennis Hall of Famer

"You're a winner when you work as hard in school as we do on the court! Stay in school! It's your best move."

Patrick Ewing
All-Star Center—New York Knicks

"Talk to your parents and teachers about AIDS. Don't be afraid to talk about it. . . . Be compassionate for the people who are infected or affected. Just because people are infected doesn't mean they're different from you."

Mary Fisher
AIDS Spokesperson, Artist, Author

"Remember: Failure is your friend. It is a major tool of progress. DARE!"

Nina Foch
Actress

"Promptness is very important. Tardiness is inexcusable in my mind. If someone asks you to do something, just do it and show your willingness to be part of a team."

Eileen Ford
Modeling Agency Executive

"I encourage you to set goals and strive for excellence in all you do. The experience, knowledge, and discipline you acquire during your youth will be an immeasurable benefit in your adult life and how you affect this nation and its people. . . . Celebrate your life by being true to yourself."

Gerald Ford
Former President of the United States

"If you make a mistake and refuse to admit it, you hurt yourself twice: once, when you make the mistake; a second time, when you refuse to learn from your mistake."

Milton Friedman
Nobel Laureate in Economics

"Do something for your fellow man. I think my generation forgot that this is a fundamental part of a democratic society."

Charles Fuller
Pulitzer Prize-winning Playwright

"Don't ever be afraid to ask questions about things you don't understand."

Kenny G
Musician

"Master the English language, both in writing and orally. You may be the smartest person but unless you can communicate effectively, you won't be successful. Keep a perspective on things. Try to have passion and purpose in your life every day. Success depends on perseverance."

Gil Garcetti
District Attorney—Los Angeles

"We make a living by what we get—we make a life by what we give."

Bill Gates
Founder, CEO—Microsoft

"Keep your word and value your reputation—it's the one thing that, once you lose it, you can't get back."

Leeza Gibbons
Television Personality

"Work and study hard, and the sky is *no* limit."

Robert Gibson
Astronaut

"It is important for young people to become involved in their communities. Keep informed of news and current events. The more informed people are about their communities, the better citizens they will be."

Rudolph Giuliani
Mayor—New York City

"The world is an exciting place and these are exciting times with endless career options. . . . Remember that the choices you make throughout your life will affect the lives of many people other than yourself. Therefore, you need to make the most responsible decisions possible."

John Glenn
Former Astronaut, United States Senator—Ohio

"Speak up and let your friends, family, and leaders know how you feel about the environment. Remember we are connected to the earth, so make an effort to educate yourself about what you can do to conserve energy, recycle, or clean up your area."

Al Gore
Vice President of the United States

"The most important thing in life is to enjoy each of its phases and try to be successful in each, rather than fantasizing about what might be."

Bob Graham
United States Senator—Florida

"**A**lways give a 100% effort in anything that you do whether it's in sports or in school. That's all anybody can ask of you, but if you don't, then you're only cheating yourself."

Horace Grant
Forward—Orlando Magic

"**I**f you can do with your life the kind of work that you take genuine pleasure in, you're going to be happy. The best way to put it is, if you want to be where you have to be when you're a grownup, you're a lucky person."

Jeff Greenfield
Author, Television News Political Commentator—"Nightline"

"Try to do what you really want to do. Don't let people tell you you can't do something if that's what you really want to do. My breakthrough came when I realized that it was funnier to tell jokes that I thought were funny than to make other people laugh. I just gave up on other people and tried to amuse myself."

Matt Groening
Creator—"The Simpsons"

"My advice is my daily motto: 'Give up the quest for perfection and shoot for five good minutes in a row.'"

Cathy Guisewite
Cartoonist—"Cathy"

"Never, never let anyone convince you to take drugs. If you do, you not only destroy yourself, but your dreams as well."

Marvin Hamlisch
Award-winning Composer

"As you grow older, always try to perceive the many great and beautiful things the world around us offers. Hold them close to your mind and heart—as defense against the ugliness and evils which are also part of our lives."

Una Hanbury
Sculptor

"**K**eep your mind and your heart open throughout your life—this is the key to everlasting youth."

Herbie Hancock
Grammy- and Oscar-winning Musician, Composer

"**I** found out early in life that the best way to get *a head* was to make one."

Duane Hanson
Artist, Creator of Lifelike Human Sculptures

"**S**tay consistent. Stay out of trouble."

Anfernee Hardaway
All-Star Guard—Orlando Magic

"In your dealings with others, do not promise more than you can deliver. Surprise on the upside, not the downside. Deliver more than you promise. This builds trust."

Paul Hardin
Chancellor—University of North Carolina

"Never go to a doctor whose office plants have died."

Tom Harkin
United States Senator—Iowa

"The most valuable thing a kid can do now is to learn to speak, write, and read the English language. Real control of the English language will take you a lot farther than a jump shot will."

Charlton Heston
Academy Award-winning Actor

"The most important message that I can deliver to kids today is that they need to listen to their parents. . . . There used to be times when I could not understand my parents and the way they disciplined me, but I now realize that they were always right, even though I did not want to believe that when I was a kid."

Grant Hill
All-Star Guard—Detroit Pistons

"My dad used to tell me, 'Check the price, son.' Check the price, kids, check the price because there is a price to be paid for whatever you do in life, whether it is good or it is bad. Before you do something, ask yourself is it worth the price you have to pay?"

Larry Holmes
Champion Heavyweight Boxer

"If we have one saying at Notre Dame that I like, it is, 'First we'll be best; then we'll be first.'" This doesn't always hold true in the polls, but it's not a bad philosophy to live by."

Lou Holtz
Football Coach—Notre Dame

"'Good'—'Better'—'Best.' Never let it rest. Until the 'Good' is 'Better' and the 'Better' is 'Best.'"

Benjamin Hooks
Civil Rights Leader, Former President—NAACP

"Make every possible effort to be fair in all your relationships with others. Never try to take advantage of anyone. Earn your success by your own efforts."

Lamar Hunt
Entrepreneur, Investor

"Winning isn't everything, but wanting to is."

Jim "Catfish" Hunter
Baseball Hall of Fame Pitcher

"I believe in the power of dreaming. In the young, dreams are the first step toward ambition; education the next. Along the way, you develop the self-confidence and inner strength necessary for success. I call them my 'suit of armor.'"

Charlayne Hunter-Gault
Television News Correspondent

"Every day commit something to memory: a poem, a saying, some new words, a foreign language. You will be rich in wisdom and wit."

Alice Ilchman
President—Sarah Lawrence College

"Words are the best weapons. Guns are for cowards."

Paul Ilyinsky
Mayor—Palm Beach, Florida

"Have mercy, forgiveness, and love for one another."

Kathy Ireland
Model, Actress

"Invention and discovery are the only true intellectual acts. Everything else is copying, reproduction, convention, laziness, and sleep. Keep trying!"

Helmut Jahn
Architect

"Don't have faith in anything without proof."

Penn Jillette
Comedian and Magician—Penn & Teller

"You are approaching that stage in life when you must take personal responsibility for your own destiny. . . . You have to learn to meet challenges and even crises. Learn to see the needs of others and have the courage to practice what you believe in."

His Holiness Pope John Paul II

"Take responsibility. It's your life. HIV happened to me, so I know it could happen to you. I want you to stay safe. Your life is worth it."

Magic Johnson
Basketball Superstar—Los Angeles Lakers

"Don't give in to peer pressure."

Chipper Jones
All-Star Third Baseman—Atlanta Braves

"Acquire the best education to allow yourself to select a proper place in life."

James Earl Jones
Actor

"Always work to improve your mind, for no one can take that away from you. This important bit of advice I received when I was a young girl. I have applied this to my life and found that it served me well."

Barbara Jordan
Former United States Congresswoman—Texas

"Take small steps. Don't let anything trip you up. All those steps are like pieces of a puzzle. They come together to form a picture. When it's complete, you've reached your ultimate goal. Step by step. I can't see any other way of accomplishing anything."

Michael Jordan
Basketball Superstar—Chicago Bulls

"If you want a helping hand, first look to the end of your own arm."

Naomi Judd
Country Singer

"Whatever you want to do with your life, whatever you strive to do, be the best you can be at it, whether it's a doctor, a garbage collector, or a baseball player."

Dave Justice
All-Star Outfielder—Atlanta Braves

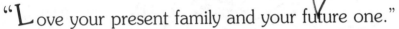

"Love your present family and your future one."

Alfred Kahn
Economist

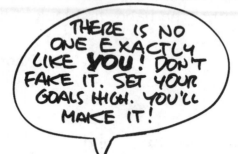

Bil Keane
Cartoonist—
"Family Circus"

"Eat breakfast! It's the most important meal of the day."

Adam Keefe
Basketball Player—Utah Jazz

"Study, study, study, and I don't just mean books. Research your family heritage, visit another religion's church, speak a foreign language, listen to your elders, study abroad, understand the stock market, participate in Junior Olympics, or get involved in a local issue. Whatever it is, take it upon yourself to learn everything you can about your community, your family, your world, and most importantly yourself."

Bob Kerrey
United States Senator—Nebraska

"Nothing in the world can take the place of persistence. Talent will not; nothing is more common than men with talent. Genius will not; unrewarded genius is almost a proverb. Education will not; the world is full of educated derelicts. Persistence and determination alone are omnipotent."

Hank Ketcham
Cartoonist—"Dennis the Menace"

"Don't try to please everybody."

Billie Jean King
Tennis Hall of Famer

"I went to school in Stanley, New Mexico, and one day the governor of New Mexico came to visit our school. . . . He said one of us might grow up to be governor one day. He was right. I have been elected governor three times. So my advice is to pursue your dreams."

Bruce King
Former Governor—New Mexico

"Trust your own instincts—don't worry if you don't know what profession you want to go into. There are many late-bloomers. Hang tough!"

Larry King
Radio and Television Talk Show Host

"Our success depends on our willingness to respect our differences. See diversity not as a threat, but as a treasure, an opportunity to enrich and strengthen the fabric of our society. Use diversity as a building block—and never as a weapon."

John Kitzhaber
Governor—Oregon

"There are several qualities that you will need to lead you down the road to a successful life. You need to have a good education, a good work ethic, a determination to achieve, and, if you come to Alaska, a warm pair of gloves."

Tony Knowles
Governor—Alaska

"Take your work seriously—and yourself not at all."

Stanley Kramer
Movie Producer

"Whatever happens in life, just remember you are in the driver's seat. Don't blame either your past, relatives, or friends for the mishaps in life. A setback is only if you allow it to become such. Some of the greatest successes are when we rise above obstacles."

Kreskin
World's Foremost Mentalist

"My formula for success:
    1. Study hard
      2. Work hard
        3. Have tall parents."

Christian Laettner
Forward—Atlanta Hawks

"Stay true to yourself, listen to your heart, and always have a dictionary on your desk."

k.d. lang
Singer

"Good ideas usually evolve out of pretty lame ones, and vice versa. 'Off days' are a part of life, whether you are a cartoonist, a neurosurgeon, or an air-traffic controller. Some ideas spring forth from just staring stupidly at a blank sheet of paper and thinking about aardvarks or toaster ovens or just about anything."

Gary Larson
Cartoonist—"The Far Side"

"In Universe time, we are here for only an instant and are each but a speck of sand. And *yet,* as we awaken each day, we must realize, 'For me the world was created.'"

Norman Lear
Television Producer, Creator—"All in the Family"

"Wanna be a superhero? All you need is great power! And knowledge is the greatest power of all. . . . So don't be a wimp! Study! Read! Learn as much as you can, because Marvel needs all the superheroes we can get!"

Stan Lee
Chairman—Marvel Films, Marvel Comics

"You never know what you can do until you try. Think of the glass as half full instead of half empty. You can do it!"

Janet Leigh
Actress

"The most important quality to have in order to be successful is dedication, but there are other qualities that you also need—they are: desire, attitude, belief, and perseverance. Stay positive and stay focused."

Sugar Ray Leonard
World Champion Boxer

"The battles don't always go to the stronger or faster man, but sooner or later the man who wins is the one who thinks he can. Never give up on your dreams."

Carl Lewis
Olympic Champion, Winner of Nine Gold Medals—Track and Field

"The day begins the night before. If you get lots of sleep you'll have lots of energy and personal power—and you'll have more fun."

Shari Lewis
Television Personality, Ventriloquist, Puppeteer

"One of the most profound things to learn is that we don't know what is possible and what is impossible. What we *do* know is that only those who are willing to follow their dream, truly have an intention to succeed, *and* are willing to risk being perceived as 'unrealistic' have any chance of making it."

Judith Light
Actress

"The highest quality in a person is tolerance of differences. Whenever we most feel that we are right and someone is wrong, we should remember that the smartest people in the world once believed that the planet was flat."

Arthur Liman
Lawyer

"One of the hard things about growing up is to actually know what you feel and think as you change. We're constantly changing. It's helpful growing up to realize that other people have felt the same emotions that you are going through."

Yo Yo Ma
Concert Cellist

"Life gets better every year."

Melissa Manchester
Singer

"Don't take things for granted. Try to treat other people like you would want to be treated."

Dan Marino
Legendary Quarterback—Miami Dolphins

"Don't be blue."

Steve Martin
Actor, Comedian

"Sticking to principles counts."

Mary McCarthy
Author

"The best idea for a young person is to set an attainable goal. . . . You attain your goal and set another attainable goal and so on. In other words, don't reach for the stars all at once—get to the top of a hill and then move on."

Ed McMahon
Television Personality

"You'll get along fine so long as you can laugh at yourself every now and then. It helps to keep things in perspective."

Walter Mears
Pulitzer Prize-winning Journalist

"One of my favorite quotes is: 'How much easier our work would be if we put forth as much effort trying to improve the quality of it as most of us do trying to find excuses for not properly attending to it.' I think these words should inspire us all to do the very best that we can in our lives."

Robert Merrill
Opera Singer

"Do not ever stop believing that you make a difference; you do. Do not ever stop believing that you can make the world a better place to live; you can. Do not ever stop believing that you have taught adults that our decisions affect your lives forever; you have."

Stephen Merrill
Governor—New Hampshire

"Every kid is unique—there never was one exactly like him before and there won't be one exactly like him again. So when you hear the word 'you,' it means something special."

Arthur Miller
Pulitzer Prize-winning Playwright

"With your drive and your dreams you can do anything and become anything you want."

Liza Minelli
Actress, Singer

"Listen to the words of your heart. Trust the words of your heart. Don't look to the world for the answers."

Michael Moriarty
Actor

"Have faith in yourself and in your own abilities."

Carol Mosely-Braun
United States Senator—Illinois

"The secret to life is giving back more than you take, and not expecting society to look after you."

Rupert Murdoch
Media Tycoon, Owner—Fox Broadcasting Network

"These words have been an inspiration to me since I was a child and I hope they will be for you as well: 'Whatever you vividly imagine, ardently desire, sincerely believe, and enthusiastically act upon, must inevitably come to pass.'"

Patty Murray
United States Senator—Washington

"Find something that you're interested in. Be passionate about it. If you don't know that word, look it up; you're behind already."

Chris Myers
Radio and Television Sports Analyst

"A true winner is a person who learns to deal with and bounce back from the tough times in life."

Tim Naehring
Infielder—Boston Red Sox

"The most important thing is to learn how to learn."

John Naisbitt
Trend Analyst, Author

"Other than emotions, your health is the most important thing. Take care of your health. Get in a proper kind of routine for exercise and growth. Start off by eating the right things. Then you can eat plenty of junk, candy bars, and ice cream. I do."

Joe Namath
Football Hall of Fame Quarterback

"The shortest way to achieve whatever you want is to do the best that you can and have fun doing it because life is not forever. So, be a kid and have a good time. Keep some of the innocence. Listen to your head but follow your heart."

Martina Navratilova
Champion Tennis Player

"Find your dream and pursue it with all your heart. Don't let disappointments along the way deter you."

Bob Newhart
Comedian, Actor

"Try to be open to and interested in just about everything life offers. Challenge yourself in every way you can think of, commit yourself to whatever it is you love to do, and don't forget to appreciate the people who help you along your way."

Jack Nicklaus
Golfer, Golf Course Designer

"Always remember—'A wet bird never flies at night!'"

Leslie Nielsen
Actor—*Naked Gun*

"I have learned through the years that all things that are truly valuable will require us to devote long study and effort, forgo many pleasures and conveniences, endure many hardships and sacrifices. Even then, there is no assurance of any reward, except that most important reward, as Ralph Waldo Emerson observed, 'The reward of a thing well done, is to have done it.'"

Sam Nunn
United States Senator—Georgia

"Be a leader, not a follower. Be yourself."

Charles Oakley
All-Star Forward—New York Knicks

"Listen when people talk but don't always take their advice because it's not always right."

John Oates
Singer, Songwriter

"Get plenty of sleep. Don't watch TV at night—not even my show. Sleep constantly. You need at least eleven hours, fourteen if you can get it."

Conan O'Brien
Television Talk Show Host

"Make excellence your habit. Do every task you undertake as well as you can, no matter how trivial the task. Give freely of yourselves always to your family, your community, and your nation."

Sandra Day O'Connor
First Woman Justice, United States Supreme Court

"You need to listen to your parents. You may not want to always do as they tell you, but they're only telling you for your own good and for what's best for you."

Shaquille O'Neal
All-Star Center—Los Angeles Lakers

"Follow your dreams! Don't let anyone tell you you can't."

"Super" Dave Osborn
Television Personality

"Expect the worst—you may sometimes get the best."

John Osborne
Award-winning Playwright

"Trust your instincts."

Frank Oz
Co-creator—The Muppets

"I try to abide by my favorite poem in both my personal and career life: 'If you think you are beaten, you are; If you think that you dare not, you don't; If you'd like to win, but you think you can't, it's almost certain you won't. If you think you'll lose, you've lost; For out in the world you'll find, success begins with a fellow's will—it's all in the state of mind.'"

Arnold Palmer
Golfer, Golf Course Designer

"Everyone living together in peace and harmony and love is the goal we all should seek."

Rosa Parks
Civil Rights Leader

"Something that has always inspired me is this quotation: 'A man's reach should exceed his grasp, or what's a heaven for?'"

Joe Paterno
Football Coach—Penn State University

"Love your parents deeply and you will learn how to take love with you into the world."

Tom Paxton
Singer

"Moderation is the key to life."

Mike Piazza
All-Star Catcher—Los Angeles Dodgers

"Never cheat to win. You don't have to cheat to be successful. In fact, you don't even have to bend your principles."

T. Boone Pickens
Entrepreneur

"Don't be afraid to try. Remember, a failed attempt is not in any way equivalent to personal failure. Some of life's sweetest successes are achieved after someone tells you, 'You can't do that!'"

Bill Pogue
Skylab Astronaut

"You can look forward to a wonderful life—make the most of it."

Christopher Reeve
Actor—*Superman*

"My mother advised me at a very early age to think carefully before making a statement, using these criteria: Is it true? Is it necessary? Is it kind? I have never regretted following her wise advice, but I have learned that ignoring her advice inevitably results in regret. Her wise words are for kids of all ages who are tempted to speak before thinking about the effects of their words."

Jerry Reinsdorf
Chairman—Chicago Bulls

"Believe in yourself and your ability to do almost anything you want to do, if it is the right thing to do. Do and say what you believe to be right, not what you think people want to hear you say. Study hard and learn to read quickly and thoroughly. Learn to write clearly and persuasively."

Janet Reno
United States Attorney General

"Stick with the optimists; it's going to be tough enough even if they're right. Don't worry too much about the future. The 21st century is probably going to be the best of them all."

James Reston
Pulitzer Prize-winning Columnist—*New York Times*

"Don't be discouraged by a setback here and there—we all have them! If I'd quit gymnastics every time I fell off the balance beam, I'd never have become an Olympic Champion. Every day that you stick with it puts you one step closer to success. *Nothing* is beyond your reach."

Mary Lou Retton
Former Olympic Champion—Gymnastics

"Stay a kid as long as you can. The best thing about being young is that you have no fear of mortality or failing, so you can do wonderful things. . . . One of the reasons that I had a fair amount of success was that I wasn't a grownup until I was forty-something."

Burt Reynolds
Actor

"Faith and trust create a higher level of results. Just because we can do better doesn't mean we have done poorly. Avoid negative people. Teamwork multiplies the potential of everyone and everything."

Jerry Richardson
Owner—Carolina Panthers

"Your imagination, your new ideas, your undreamed-of dreams will bring about the discoveries of tomorrow. Instead of reading textbooks, you'll be writing them with the history of what you've done. What could be more exciting than that? Never underestimate the power of learning. It's our greatest gift."

William Richardson
President—Johns Hopkins University

"Being able to read enhances everyone's life. Not only will it open many doors for you, but it will also broaden your horizons. It's an adventure every time you open a book."

Cal Ripken, Jr.
All-Star Shortstop—Baltimore Orioles

"Our survival depends on each of us creatively finding our own ways to deal with our anger—ways that don't hurt others or ourselves. There's a very good feeling in being able to control 'the mad that you feel'—no matter how old we are."

Fred Rogers
Television Personality—"Mister Rogers' Neighborhood"

"Insofar as children are open to anything, they are artists. . . . Do not let grown-ups drain you of poetry and imagination by urging you to think mostly of money as you reach adolescence, for then there is no turning back. Money is just a means to an end, but art is an end in itself."

Ned Rorem
Pulitzer Prize-winning Composer, Author

"Work hard! Don't depend on luck."

Rita Rudner
Comedienne

"Don't watch so much TV. . . . It can turn you into an unmotivated robot. Beevis and Butthead can be funny, but not if you are just like them—especially the hair."

Bob Saget
Comedian, Actor,
Television Host—"America's Funniest Home Videos"

"Take advantage of every opportunity that will present itself and even create some of your own, to give back to society some of the riches into which you were born."

Jonas Salk, M.D.
Inventor of the Polio Vaccine

"You just gotta believe. You've got to believe in yourself. If you don't believe in yourself, nobody else will."

Deion Sanders
Pro Bowl Football Player—Dallas Cowboys

"Indifference is often the easy way out, but it takes courage to care enough to commit. Be creative and inspire others to follow your lead. As Emerson said, 'What a new face courage puts on everything!'"

Vidal Sassoon
Hair Products Executive

"My motto has always been, 'Take advantage of opportunities as they arise.'"

Patricia Schroeder
United States Congresswoman—Colorado

"Learn to save money. Every successful person has learned the fundamental rule of saving money to invest in his or her long-term future. As young people, you can get a headstart by putting away part of your allowance or money received for part-time jobs. You will be amazed at how quickly your savings grow over the years."

Charles Schwab
Stock Brokerage Executive

"The scientific discoverer is the first to see or know a *really* new thing. She or he is the locksmith of the centuries who has finally fashioned a key to open the door to one of nature's secrets. . . . The possibilities are almost limitless. And *you* can be a part of it."

Glenn Seaborg
Nobel Laureate in Chemistry

"Always try to do the right thing. It's important to believe in yourself and have faith. Always try to follow your goals because anything is achievable if you put your mind to it."

Seal
Singer, Songwriter

"Most grownups try, but they really are stupid, trying to get rich or famous or something. You know: The important thing is to have fun with your friends and not hurt anybody, even if they are not your friend. You never know."

Pete Seeger
Folk Singer

"Think about how lucky you are to have been born at all. The odds against that are so mind-boggling it's a miracle any of us ever got here. So while you're at it, you may as well try to make your life count for something you believe in."

Artie Shaw
Bandleader

"The secret to success is to always take pride in what you do, and do more than you are expected to do."

Sidney Sheldon
Novelist

"Drink lots of milk because it's good for the bones. Put a lot of Vitamin E around your eyes so you don't get crow's feet. Try and do a lot of situps because girls don't like guys with big bellies. Try and find something that you want to see yourself doing when you're sixty."

Pauly Shore
Comedian, Actor

"Follow your gut, be willing to work extremely hard, and never be afraid to fail. All great people have failed in their lives. . . . It's how you find out what you're made of. But always remember that no job is more important than your family."

Maria Shriver
Television Journalist

"Make the most out of every moment. Whatever you're doing, just enjoy it. Be the best you can. If you can do that, then a lot of good things will happen to you in your life."

Don Shula
Legendary Football Coach—Miami Dolphins

"Follow the example of people who live fulfilled lives and who have earned your respect by the way they treat you and others."

John Silber
President—Boston University

"Life is a funny thing—the harder you work, the luckier you get."

Melvin Simon
Real Estate Magnate, Owner—Indiana Pacers

"Be cool. Act smooth. Hang loose."

Brian Skrudland
Hockey Player—Florida Panthers

"Keep your chin up, your chest out, and never ever let your enemy eat your breakfast. Say no to drugs, and that's an order."

Sergeant Slaughter
Wrestler, Television Personality

"Don't go into your father's business unless you know he's going to leave it to you and you're going to make a lot of money. Get through high school. . . . Then you can lie on your résumé about college because nobody looks it up."

Bobby Slayton
Comedian

"The best advice I received was in the form of a prayer: 'Dear God, give me the strength to accept the things I cannot change, the courage to change the things I can, and the wisdom to know the difference.'"

Dean Smith
Hall of Fame Basketball Coach—
University of North Carolina

"Every human being is entitled to courtesy and consideration. Constructive criticism is not only to be expected but sought. Smears are not only to be expected but fought. Honor is to be earned but not bought."

Margaret Chase Smith
First Female United States Senator

"Don't hesitate to ask questions; it is no disgrace to admit your ignorance. . . . Small but necessary chores should be disposed of promptly. The big jobs go faster if these small jobs are not lurking in the background. Don't waste a lot of time watching TV."

George Snell
Nobel Laureate in Physiology/Medicine

"Don't take the advice of anyone who has made his life into an outrageous mess—you can probably do that just as well on your own and will have more fun doing it that way."

W. D. Snodgrass
Pulitzer Prize-winning Poet

"I'll have to be excused from contributing my advice. I doubt the wisdom of anything I might say, and the older I get the less inclined I am to give advice."

David Souter
United States Supreme Court Justice

"Mow the lawn. Make your bed. Pay your parents back for the good keep they've given you throughout your lifetime."

Warren Spahn
Baseball Hall of Fame Pitcher

"Follow your dream. Don't give up no matter what! You may not achieve all that you dream of, but a portion of a dream is a dream come true."

Aaron Spelling
Television Producer

"Take my advice: Don't take advice from strangers. I've gotten, and given, very sound advice many times over the decades, but we all seem to insist on making our own mistakes. . . . If you were to insist on hearing my advice, out of contrariness, or idle curiosity, or perhaps desperation, I'd advise you to learn how to think—never let others do it for you."

Art Spiegelman
Pulitzer Prize-winning Cartoonist—"Maus"

"The man who says 'It can't be done' is always interrupted by the man who just did it!"

Mickey Spillane
Mystery Writer

"Trust yourself! You know more than you think you do!"

Benjamin Spock, M.D.
Pediatrician, Author

"Make your dreams come true."

Sylvester Stallone
Actor

"Early to bed, early to rise. Work like the devil. And advertise."

Willie Stargell
Baseball Hall of Famer—Pittsburgh Pirates

"The strongest people in the world (including children) are those who know the difference between right and wrong and choose right despite the advice and objections of 'friends.' Be strong!"

Paul Stein
Lieutenant General—U.S. Air Force,
Superintendent—U.S. Air Force Academy

"Always respect and love your parents. . . . Do whatever your parents say. They are your best friends in life. Don't ever forget that."

George Steinbrenner
Owner—New York Yankees

"The wisest thing you can do is to be able to take the best out of what people tell you and put it into yourself as part of your own life. Never be afraid to ask questions, and never be afraid to find out why people came to say what they want to tell you. Because when they try to explain, you'll learn even more."

Isaac Stern
Concert Violinist

"Be a giver, not just a taker."

Ezra Stone
Producer, Director, Actor

"Be true to yourself."

Sharon Stone
Actress

"Don't be afraid to take risks. . . . If you aren't willing to take risks, you won't ever fail—but you also won't ever succeed."

Don Sundquist
Governor—Tennessee

"When I was growing up, they taught us the three R's—reading, writing, and 'rithmetic. I would love to see kids today build their young lives on three R's, too—reality, responsibility, and relationships."

Don Sutton
Former All-Star Pitcher—Los Angeles Dodgers

"Anyone can have a great idea. Only a few people ever work hard to turn an idea into reality. If we learn how to work hard, more than ideas become reality. Dreams will come true."

Lynn Swann
Football Hall of Famer—Pittsburgh Steelers

"To love is to give and to give is to love."

Elizabeth Taylor
Academy Award-winning Actress

"Know when to shut up. It can be very worthwhile."

Teller
Comedian and Magician—Penn & Teller

"Know that you are a special person, unique from anyone else, and that you have been blessed with qualities that you can use to reach your goals and to make the world around you a better place."

Isiah Thomas
Former All-Star Guard—Detroit Pistons

"My mother always told me, 'Seize the moment of excited curiosity.' In other words—go for it."

Michael Tilson Thomas
Orchestra Conductor

"I offer these words of advice that my father gave to me when I first entered politics: 'You have two ears and one mouth. Use them in that proportion and you'll go far in life.'"

Tommy Thompson
Governor—Wisconsin

"Stay healthy. Be happy. The healthier you are the happier you are."

Cheryl Tiegs
Model

"As my grandfather used to say—'Don't complain about your taxes. Remember they are your dues to the best club in the world.'"

Nina Totenberg
Commentator—National Public Radio

"Respect and love your parents."

John Travolta
Actor

"Don't be afraid or intimidated by the fact that you have to pay your dues in life and work hard before you achieve success. If you've got something that you really want to do, persevere and it will pay off."

Alex Trebek
Television Host—"Jeopardy"

"Study, learn, and grow so your work can help others—whether in your school, striving to help the environment, or encouraging understanding of people different from yourself. If everybody everywhere made a small effort to improve his or her corner of the world, it would make a tremendous difference."

Ted Turner
Owner—CNN, TBS, TNT, Atlanta Braves, Atlanta Hawks

"Be brief. Never use words that may not be understood by everyone. Keep your sentences short, and to communicate clearly, keep it simple."

Abigail Van Buren
Columnist—"Dear Abby"

"Read! A book can be as delicious as a hot-fudge sundae, as exciting as a roller-coaster ride, and as beautiful as a spring morning."

Judith Viorst
Author, Poet

"Above all, enjoy life, look around you, be curious, and don't ever take no for an answer. Live your life like a journey and take advantage of all the scenery, even the not so pleasant."

Diane Von Furstenberg
Fashion Designer

"Develop a sense of humor. Try to see the funny side of what happens to you. . . . A person who has a sense of humor is agreeable to others and good company. His or her humor will help soften a lot of hard knocks in life and put experiences into the proper perspective."

Mort Walker
Cartoonist—"Beetle Bailey"

"Good things happen to good people. If you make the right decisions in life, good things will happen to you."

Steve Walsh
Quarterback—St. Louis Rams

"A great man once said: 'If each person swept in front of his or her own doorstep the world would be a perfect place.' Take care of your own life first in order to make a difference in the world."

Andre Watts
Concert Pianist

"Identify your talents, yourself or with the help of others, and then carefully develop and nurture them. It will help you earn your living, contribute to your happiness and self-respect, and be good for the country."

Byron White
Former United States Supreme Court Justice

"You should always listen to your parents. I know sometimes it seems they don't know what they are talking about, but actually they have probably experienced the same thing so they have learned from experience. Remember, they are only looking out for *your* best interests!"

Vanna White
Television Personality—"Wheel of Fortune"

"Make doing something nice for someone else a part of your daily routine. The rewards from an unselfish act of kindness are tremendous."

Andy Williams
Singer

"Make fun, not war."

Robin Williams
Actor, Comedian

"Have a belief in yourself that is bigger than anyone's disbelief."

August Wilson
Poet, Pulitzer Prize-winning Playwright

"It's very important to dream BIG dreams and work hard toward reaching your dreams. You can achieve all of your dreams through knowledge, but also know that you can only gain knowledge through education. Work hard in school. Keep up your grades. Excellent grades are the key to great success."

Oprah Winfrey
Television Talk Show Host

"Self-respect is cool. So are you."

Henry Winkler
Producer, Director, Actor

"Each one of us has unique gifts or talents, and our lives will be easier and happier if we make the most of those. Also, don't worry so much about what others think of you. Do what you think is right, and you'll be just fine."

Judy Woodruff
Television News Anchor—CNN

"Always tell the truth."

James Woods
Actor

"If you love your work, you will be successful—that applies to schoolwork, creative work, or your work when you're an adult. But success is not only measured in dollars. When you love your work, it's measured in a vision, a dream, personal fulfillment, a sense of peace, service, and purpose."

Peter Yarrow
Singer—Peter, Paul & Mary

"My best advice is to do what you are told. Obedience is a neglected virtue. Parents, if they don't always know best, have a much higher batting average than their offspring."

Robert Young
Actor—"Father Knows Best"